Stanislaus Mouse
Learns How to Fly

Written by Joe Gornall
Illustrated by Ken Roberts

PRICE STERN SLOAN
Los Angeles

Library of Congress Cataloging-in-Publication Data

Gornall, Joe, 1928–
  Stanislaus mouse learns how to fly.

  Summary: A clumsy mouse wins the respect of the other mice when an owl
teaches him how to use his tremendous sneezing ability in order to fly.
  [1. Mice—Fiction. 2. Flight—Fiction 3. Sneeze—Fiction] I. Roberts, Ken, ill.
II. Title. PZ7.G6724St 1988   [E]   87-32801
                      ISBN 0-8431-2224-2

Copyright © 1987 by Joe Gornall
Published by Price Stern Sloan, Inc.
360 North La Cienega Boulevard, Los Angeles, California 90048

ISBN: 0-8431-2224-2

There is a mouse named Stanislaus
  Who can blow himself up just as big as a house.
How does he do it, so tiny and thin?
  Instead of sneezing out, he sneezes in!

It all began back when Stanislaus was a teeny tiny baby mouse. Father Mouse accidentally dropped pollen from his alfalfa sprig into Stanislaus's nose.

  "Oops!" said Father.

  "Poor dear!" said Mother, "Now he's going to sneeze."

All of a sudden, strange sounds were heard
from the crib. They sounded like sneezes,
but not quite the same.

"Gracious!" exclaimed Mother, "He's sneezing
in instead of *out!*"

"Impossible!" said Father.

To Mother and Father's amazement,
Baby Stanislaus began to blow up just like
a balloon each time he sneezed. Soon,
he had outgrown his crib and was
bulging through the slats.

"He'll burst!" cried Mother.

"He's going to explode!"
yelled Father.

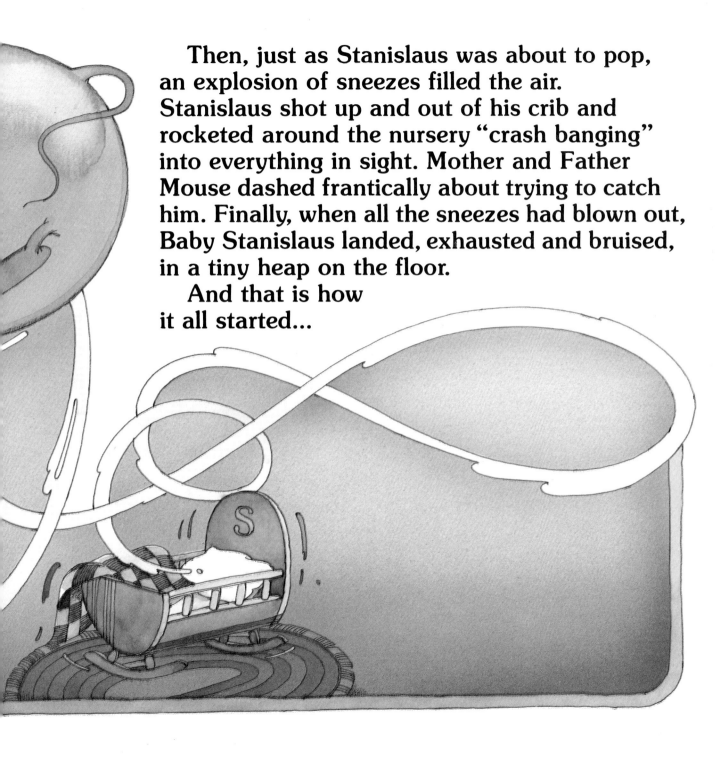

Then, just as Stanislaus was about to pop,
an explosion of sneezes filled the air.
Stanislaus shot up and out of his crib and
rocketed around the nursery "crash banging"
into everything in sight. Mother and Father
Mouse dashed frantically about trying to catch
him. Finally, when all the sneezes had blown out,
Baby Stanislaus landed, exhausted and bruised,
in a tiny heap on the floor.

And that is how
it all started...

Many years later on a bright, sunny summer day all the children mice were outside playing games. Stanislaus wanted to play, too. But, as usual, the children pushed him away and called him stupid names.

"Clumsy, clumsy Stanislaus Mouse, clumsy old mouse as big as a house!" they shouted. "You can't play. You'll just sneeze and wreck everything in sight!" Soon a crowd gathered and a big, rough, gruff voice shouted, "Let's make him sneeze!"

It was the voice of Meany Mouse, the biggest, nastiest mouse of them all.

"Yeah, yeah!" echoed the crowd. "Let's make him sneeze, let's make him sneeze!"

"Oh no!" cried Stanislaus as he tried to run away. Quickly, he was thrown to the ground and held down tightly. Meany Mouse stepped forward. He was laughing.

"Don't make me sneeze," pleaded Stanislaus, "please don't."

But Meany Mouse just continued laughing as he kicked dust up poor Stanislaus's nose. "Bye-bye, Clumsy!" he laughed, "Have a nice flight!"

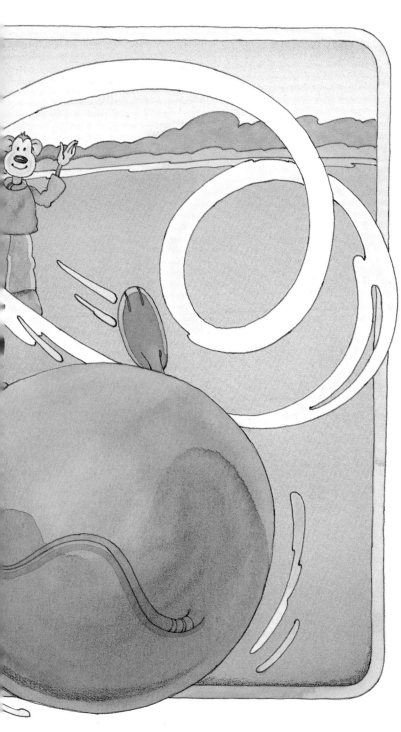

Stanislaus began to sneeze. He sneezed and he sneezed and he sneezed. He sneezed *in* instead of *out* and blew himself up just as big as a house. Then, just as he was about to go "boom," all those sneezes roared out of his nose in one huge "whoosh!" Stanislaus shot up into the sky, tumbling and twisting like an old rag doll.

"Have a nice flight!" shouted the crowd. They laughed sarcastically and waved good-bye.

Poor Stanislaus zoomed up and up and up and up until he was just a tiny dot in the sky. When the sneezes finally blew themselves out, Stanislaus floated to earth and landed "plop!" right in the evergreen tree where wise Orville Owl was taking his afternoon nap.

"HOOOOOOT!" exclaimed a startled Orville, smoothing his ruffled feathers. "When you drop in for a visit, you really drop in."

"Sorry, Mr. Orville," said Stanislaus, trying to catch his breath. "I have this sneezing problem that sends me flying, and I never know where I'm going to land."

"Well, my young friend," said Orville, "everyone has problems now and then. It's how you handle them that's important."

"But none of the other kids has my problem," said Stanislaus. "None of them gets pushed away and called stupid names. None of them gets laughed at and made fun of."

Stanislaus's lips began to tremble, and soon big tears were rolling down his tiny cheeks. Poor Stanislaus began to sob and he hid his face between his knees so Orville couldn't see how unhappy he really was.

"I'm going to run away where I'll never be able to wreck anything again," he sputtered, "and they'll never *ever* have to put up with clumsy old Stanislaus anymore!"

Wise Orville Owl knelt down beside him and put his big feathered wing around Stanislaus's shaking shoulders. "Hold on my friend," he said softly, " no need to cry. Problems are only temporary. They can all be solved, you know. And I can help you solve yours."

"You can help me stop sneezing *in* instead of *out*?" asked Stanislaus, wiping the tears from his eyes.

"No," answered Orville, "but I can help you control your flights."

"Really?" asked Stanislaus. "But, how?"

"Well," said Orville, puffing up his chest, "I can teach you how to fly. We owls are good fliers, you know."

"Fly...me fly? You mean I could learn to soar and glide and turn and bank and take off and land and...and..." sputtered Stanislaus excitedly.

"Yes, and much, much more. Are you interested?" asked Orville Owl.

"I am, I am!" shouted Stanislaus.

"Will you listen very carefully and practice what I teach you?" asked Orville sternly.

"I will, I will!" promised Stanislaus.

"Good, then we'll make a plan." Owls always make plans because that's a wise thing to do. "Our plan," said Orville Owl, "will be a secret plan." Secret plans, you see, are a lot more fun than just plain old plans.

Then, whispering very softly so that no one could hear, Orville Owl told Stanislaus to meet him every night up in the hay mow of the farmer's barn.

"There's lots of chaff there to make you sneeze," he said, "and plenty of nice soft hay to cushion your falls. OK?"

"OK!" shouted Stanislaus so loudly that all in the woods could hear. "That's a great secret plan...let's start tonight!"

Every night from then on, while everyone was asleep, Stanislaus met Orville Owl up in the farmer's hay mow. He practiced over and over again everything Orville had taught him. It was hard work, but Stanislaus stuck with it and he never, never gave up. Soon, little by little, Stanislaus learned how to fly.

Later that same summer the mice children were enjoying another day at the playground, but they still wouldn't let Stanislaus join them. Meany Mouse kicked dust up his nose, just like before. Everyone laughed as Stanislaus sneezed *in* instead of *out* and blew himself up — just as big as a house! Then, just as he was about to burst, sure enough, the familiar "whoosh" of sneezes escaped from his twitching nose. Stanislaus blasted off, tumbling and twisting up and up and up, just as he always had before.

The crowd roared with glee. "Have a nice flight, Clumsy!" they chanted. "Bye-bye," they waved. But suddenly, their laughter stopped and a strange silence fell over the crowd. As they watched, Stanislaus slowly spread his arms and legs out just like wings. Then he rolled over and power-dived straight at the astonished mice, who scurried for cover.

Meany Mouse was not only the biggest and nastiest mouse, he was also the slowest. Before he could reach a safe hiding place, Stanislaus zoomed by and bumped Meany Mouse and he went, head over heels, "splosh" right into an icky mud puddle. "Oooh, oooh, oooh!" he bellowed as the cold, grimy mud soaked through his overalls.

Stanislaus pulled up and spiraled gracefully skyward where he performed a spectacular aerobatic display of loops, rolls and lazy eights. Well, the mice below were paralyzed with wonder and awe.

"Oooooh, aaaaah, wow, weeeee!" they murmured. Stanislaus flew down and executed a perfect stand-up landing. The amazed mice rushed to greet him. They whistled, they cheered, they clapped, they hugged him and patted him on the back. Confetti filled the air and a band played. Strains of "He's A

Jolly Good Fellow" were heard every-
where. Even Meany Mouse, covered with mud
from head to toe, rushed to greet him.
Meany Mouse hoisted Stanislaus onto his big,
brawny shoulders and proudly pranced him
about for everyone to see.

Mother and Father Mouse cried with
happiness. Wise Orville
Owl watched

from his perch in the evergreen tree. He proudly puffed
out his chest feathers, winked and smugly nodded his
approval. "HOOOOOT! HOOOOOT!" he cooed.

Well, that's the way it happened. Stanislaus became
friends with the other mice, and now he is known
worldwide as Stanislaus the Flying Mouse.